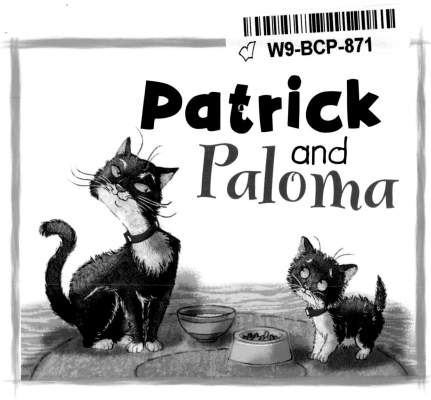

Patrick and Paloma

Lee Aucoin, *Creative Director*
Jamey Acosta, *Senior Editor*
Heidi Fiedler, *Editor*
Produced and designed by
Denise Ryan & Associates
Illustration © John Nez
Rachelle Cracchiolo, *Publisher*

Teacher Created Materials
5301 Oceanus Drive
Huntington Beach, CA 92649-1030
http://www.tcmpub.com
Paperback: ISBN: 978-1-4333-5532-5
Library Binding: ISBN: 978-1-4807-1700-8
© 2014 Teacher Created Materials
Printed in China
Nordica.072018.CA21800843

Written by Michael McMahon
Illustrated by John Nez

Patrick curled up on his favorite chair on the porch. He closed his eyes. *Ah! This is the life*, he said to himself.

Patrick liked his comfortable life. He liked his chair with its soft cushion. He liked his meals served at the same time every day. He liked his bowl of warm milk every morning.

5

One day, his owner Paz gave him a new red collar. It looked snazzy against his shiny black coat. "How handsome I look," Patrick meowed.

Patrick wondered why he was getting a new collar. It wasn't his birthday. It wasn't Paz's birthday. What was going on?

8

Then, out of the corner of his eye, he saw
a little black ball of fluff. What was it?
Oh, no! A kitten!

"Patrick, come and meet your new friend.
Her name is Paloma," said Paz.

11

Patrick wasn't pleased. He didn't need
a friend. He didn't need a silly, fluffy kitten
that ran around annoying everyone!
And Paloma was *very* annoying.

13

She jumped onto Patrick's favorite chair when he wasn't looking. She drank his milk before he was awake. She even had her evening meal before he did!

15

Patrick didn't know what to do. "Look at her running around just because she had her milk before me! And she looks so silly wearing that pink collar," he grumbled. He looked for a place to curl up and hide.

When Paloma went into the garden, Patrick thought, *Ah! It's so much better when she's not here. Now I can think about what I am going to do. Things cannot remain as they are!* Then, he settled into his cushion and started to think.

19

What if I meowed loudly at her? he thought. But he had done that already. She hadn't noticed.

Maybe I could demand to be fed in the middle of the day. Then, he remembered that Paloma was always fed in the middle of the day. "Oh! Life has become so difficult," he sighed.

One day, Paloma started to scratch at his chair. "Mew. Mew. Mew." she cried very softly, as she jumped up onto his cushion.

"Go away, Paloma!" grumbled Patrick, as he turned away. But Paloma curled up next to him and went to sleep. "Purr. Purr. Purr," she said.

"Mmm...maybe she is not as bad as I thought," said Patrick as he tried to smile. "She is a rather nice little kitten. Purr. Purr. Purr."